BELGICA

GAULISH VILLAGE

COMPENDIUM

LAUDANUM

AQUARIUM

TOTORUM

LUTETIA

ARMORICA

GAUL
(ROMAN CONQUEST)
50 BC

CELTICA

AQUITANIA

PROVINCIA

THE YEAR IS 50 BC. GAUL IS ENTIRELY OCCUPIED BY THE
ROMANS. WELL, NOT ENTIRELY ... ONE SMALL VILLAGE OF
INDOMITABLE GAULS STILL HOLDS OUT AGAINST THE INVADERS.
AND LIFE IS NOT EASY FOR THE ROMAN LEGIONARIES WHO
GARRISON THE FORTIFIED CAMPS OF TOTORUM, AQUARIUM,
LAUDANUM AND COMPENDIUM ...

ASTERIX, THE HERO OF THESE ADVENTURES. A SHREWD, CUNNING LITTLE WARRIOR, ALL PERILOUS MISSIONS ARE IMMEDIATELY ENTRUSTED TO HIM. ASTERIX GETS HIS SUPERHUMAN STRENGTH FROM THE MAGIC POTION BREWED BY THE DRUID GETAFIX . . .

OBELIX, ASTERIX'S INSEPARABLE FRIEND. A MENHIR DELIVERY MAN BY TRADE, ADDICTED TO WILD BOAR. OBELIX IS ALWAYS READY TO DROP EVERYTHING AND GO OFF ON A NEW ADVENTURE WITH ASTERIX – SO LONG AS THERE'S WILD BOAR TO EAT, AND PLENTY OF FIGHTING. HIS CONSTANT COMPANION IS DOGMATIX, THE ONLY KNOWN CANINE ECOLOGIST, WHO HOWLS WITH DESPAIR WHEN A TREE IS CUT DOWN.

GETAFIX, THE VENERABLE VILLAGE DRUID, GATHERS MISTLETOE AND BREWS MAGIC POTIONS. HIS SPECIALITY IS THE POTION WHICH GIVES THE DRINKER SUPERHUMAN STRENGTH. BUT GETAFIX ALSO HAS OTHER RECIPES UP HIS SLEEVE . . .

CACOFONIX, THE BARD. OPINION IS DIVIDED AS TO HIS MUSICAL GIFTS. CACOFONIX THINKS HE'S A GENIUS. EVERY-ONE ELSE THINKS HE'S UNSPEAKABLE. BUT SO LONG AS HE DOESN'T SPEAK, LET ALONE SING, EVERYBODY LIKES HIM . . .

FINALLY, VITALSTATISTIX, THE CHIEF OF THE TRIBE. MAJESTIC, BRAVE AND HOT-TEMPERED, THE OLD WARRIOR IS RESPECTED BY HIS MEN AND FEARED BY HIS ENEMIES. VITALSTATISTIX HIMSELF HAS ONLY ONE FEAR, HE IS AFRAID THE SKY MAY FALL ON HIS HEAD TOMORROW. BUT AS HE ALWAYS SAYS, TOMORROW NEVER COMES.

GOSCINNY AND UDERZO
PRESENT
An Asterix Adventure

ASTERIX
THE
GLADIATOR

Written by RENÉ GOSCINNY *and Illustrated by* ALBERT UDERZO

Translated by Anthea Bell *and* Derek Hockridge

© 1964 GOSCINNY/UDERZO

Revised edition and English translation © 2004 HACHETTE
Original title: *Astérix Gladiateur*

Exclusive licensee: Orion Publishing Group
Translators: Anthea Bell and Derek Hockridge
Typography: Bryony Newhouse

This revised edition first published in Great Britain by Orion Publishing Group

This edition first published in 2004 by Orion Books Ltd,
Orion House, 5 Upper Saint Martin's Lane, London WC2H 9EA

3 5 7 9 10 8 6 4

Printed in France by Partenaires

http://gb.asterix.com
www.orionbooks.co.uk

A CIP record for this book is available from the British Library

ISBN-13 978 0 75286 610 9 (cased)
ISBN-10 0 75286 610 9 (cased)
ISBN-13 978 0 75286 611 6 (paperback)
ISBN-10 0 75286 611 7 (paperback)

Distributed in the United States of America by Sterling Publishing Co. Inc.
387 Park Avenue South, New York, NY 10016

THE ROMAN CAMP OF COMPENDIUM IS IN A FERMENT. THE PREFECT OF GAUL, ODIUS ASPARAGUS, IS PAYING A CALL ON CENTURION GRACCHUS ARMISURPLUS. THE PREFECT ARRIVES FROM THE NEARBY COAST WHERE HIS GALLEY HAS PUT IN...

PRESENT... PILUM!...

AVE, PREFECT! THIS IS A GREAT HONOUR FOR ME!

AVE, CENTURION! YOU'RE TELLING ME!

AND NOW FOR THE PURPOSE OF MY VISIT, CENTURION! I'M GOING TO ROME ON LEAVE, AND CUSTOM DECREES THAT I TAKE CAESAR A HANDSOME PRESENT... SOMETHING UNUSUAL AND VERY VALUABLE...

...I DID THINK OF TAKING HIM A PRESENT FROM LUTETIA, MAYBE A MARBLE MEMO TABLET FOR HIM TO CARVE DOWN HIS APPOINTMENTS, BUT THAT'S TOO ORDINARY...

THEN I HAD A BRILLIANT IDEA! WHY NOT TAKE CAESAR ONE OF THE INVINCIBLE GAULS FROM HEREABOUTS?

WHAT?!

BUT, PREFECT, ABOUT THESE INVINCIBLE GAULS... THERE'S JUST ONE SNAG!

WELL, WHAT IS IT?

THEY HAPPEN TO BE INVINCIBLE!

THAT'S WHAT MAKES THEM SO VALUABLE! GET ME ONE OF THESE GAULS, AND YOU WON'T REGRET IT!

THERE'S CERTAINLY ONE WHO'S A BIT MORE HARMLESS THAN THE OTHERS... CACOFONIX THE BARD. HE OFTEN GOES FOR WALKS IN THE FOREST BY HIMSELF LOOKING FOR INSPIRATION!

EXCELLENT! I MUST HAVE THIS BARD – AND FAST!

AND IN THE GAULISH VILLAGE...

GOODBYE, ASTERIX, I'M GOING FOR A WALK IN THE FOREST!

GOODBYE, CACOFONIX!

5

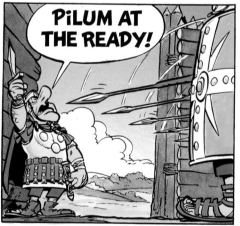

THE BATTLE IS SHORT...

BANG! CLINK CLANK CLONK! BIFF!

BUT SHARP...

SWOOOSH!

I CAN'T FIND CACOFONIX ANYWHERE... AH, THERE'S THE ROMAN COMMANDER!

BANG! BING!

I SHALL FIGHT TO THE DEATH!

WANT ME TO THUMP YOU?

OH ALL RIGHT! ALL IS LOST! I SURRENDER! ALEA JACTA EST!

AND LET IT BE A LESSON TO YOU! NOW, GIVE US BACK OUR BARD, AND DON'T DO IT AGAIN!

THE FACT IS... YOUR BARD ISN'T HERE ANY MORE. AT THIS MOMENT HE'S ON BOARD A GALLEY, SAILING FOR ROME TO BE GIVEN TO CAESAR AS A PRESENT...

!!!

WE'RE WASTING OUR TIME...

A PRESENT? THAT'S A REALLY FUNNY IDEA!

LOOK AT THIS, ASTERIX! I'M SURE I'VE WON OUR BET! AND ONE LEGIONARY WAS FIGHTING BARE-HEADED TOO. IT'S AGAINST ALL THE RULES OF WARFARE TO GO INTO BATTLE IMPROPERLY DRESSED! I'VE A GOOD MIND TO REPORT HIM!

THE GAULS WITHDRAW, LEAVING BEHIND THEM THE AFTERMATH OF BATTLE...

THEY REALLY LET US HAVE IT, EH, SIR?

IN THE FIRST PLACE, GET THIS CAMP BACK INTO ORDER!!! WHAT'S ALL THIS UNTIDINESS IN AID OF? AND DON'T ANYONE EVER MENTION THIS BATTLE TO ME AGAIN!!!

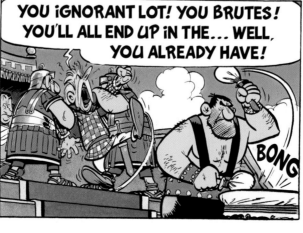

12

13

NOW TO STOP THIS SHIP SAILING ALONG THE COAST!

ASTERIX AND OBELIX MAKE THE ANCIENT GAULISH SIGN INDICATING A WISH TO BE TAKEN ON BOARD. NOTE THE FOUR CLENCHED FINGERS AND THE THUMB JERKED IN THE DESIRED DIRECTION. IF YOU WISH TO GO TO ROME, THE DIRECTION OF THE THUMB IS IMMATERIAL, SINCE ALL ROADS LEAD THERE.

N.B. THIS GESTURE IS STILL EMPLOYED TODAY, THOUGH NOT OFTEN TO STOP SHIPS.

IT'S A PHOENICIAN GALLEY. THE PHOENICIANS ARE FAMOUS SAILORS AND MERCHANTS!

WHAT'S THE PHOENICIAN FOR SINGULARIS PORCUS?

WE'RE FROM TYRE IN PHOENICIA. MY NAME IS EKONOMIKRISIS. WOULD YOU LIKE TO BUY ANY GLASS, JEWELS, TEXTILES, PURPLE, FURNITURE?

NO, WE WANT TO GO TO ROME.

HM... ER... ALL RIGHT, COME ON BOARD!

ARE THOSE SLAVES?

OH NO, THEY'RE PARTNERS... WHEN WE FLOATED THE COMPANY, I DREW UP THE CONTRACT AND THEY FAILED TO READ IT CAREFULLY BEFORE SIGNING. I'M CHAIRMAN AND MANAGING DIRECTOR.

IT'S KIND OF YOU TO TAKE US TO ROME. I HOPE IT DOESN'T MEAN GOING OUT OF YOUR WAY?

AS IT HAPPENS, WE WERE PLANNING TO GO TO ROME. ONE OF MY PREDECESSORS ABANDONED HIS SHIP THERE...

IT SANK?

NO, HE SOLD IT. HE WAS A BETTER SALESMAN THAN SAILSMAN.

16

YOU HAVE SAVED WHAT IS DEAREST TO OUR HEARTS – OUR CARGO! NOW WE'RE BOSOM FRIENDS!

I ORIGINALLY INTENDED TO SELL YOU AS SLAVES WHEN WE CALLED AT THE NEXT PORT. BUT NOW I'LL TAKE YOU TO ROME AS AGREED.

YOU CERTAINLY DO HAVE BUSINESS ACUMEN!

WHAT CAN YOU EXPECT? AS I WAS SAYING TO MY PARTNERS, WE'RE ALL IN THE SAME BOAT, AND WE MUSTN'T REST ON OUR OARS IF OUR OVERHEADS ARE NOT TO MAKE US GO UNDER!

MEANWHILE, IN ROME...

AVE, CAESAR!

AVE, ODIUS ASPARAGUS, PREFECT OF GAUL.

HERE'S MY PRESENT, O CAESAR! A GAULISH BARD FROM THE TRIBE OF INDOMITABLE GAULS IN THE COMPENDIUM AREA.

I'VE BEEN BROUGHT HERE AS A SOUVENIR... JUST AS IF I WAS A VULGAR PAINTED SHELL!

A BARD? HOW INTERESTING!

YOU CAN WAIT TILL THE COWS COME HOME BEFORE I'LL SING FOR YOU... AND YOU DON'T KNOW WHAT YOU'RE MISSING!

THANKS FOR THIS ORIGINAL LITTLE PRESENT, PREFECT. YOU MAY GO!

SEND FOR CAIUS FATUOUS, THE LANISTA. *

SNAP

* TRAINER OF THE GLADIATORS

CAIUS FATUOUS, CAN YOU MAKE A GLADIATOR OF THIS BARD?

DEAR ME, NO, O CAESAR! HE'S TOO WEAK... NOT ENOUGH MEAT ON HIM.

IF I WASN'T RESTRAINING MYSELF...

VERY WELL THEN, THROW HIM TO THE LIONS AT THE NEXT GAMES, TAKE HIM AWAY!

WELL, SO WE'VE GOT A DATE AT INSTANTMIX'S PLACE THIS EVENING. WHAT DO WE DO TILL THEN?

WE COULD GO BACK AND HAVE SOME MORE BOAR?

BOAR ON THE SPIT

THE BATHS! I'VE OFTEN HEARD ABOUT THE ROMAN BATHS! LET'S GO AND HAVE A BATH!

THERMAE

GO AND GET UNDRESSED IN THE APODYTERIA.

THAT MUST MEAN THE CHANGING ROOM...

THIS WAY, NOBLE LORDS!

IS IT US HE MEANS?

APODYTERIA

WE HAVEN'T GOT MUCH ON. I HOPE WE DON'T CATCH COLD!

SVDATORIA

IT'S HOT IN HERE!

I WONDER IF WE COULD OPEN A WINDOW.

LOOK, CAIUS FATUOUS! YOU'RE ALWAYS ON THE LOOKOUT FOR GLADIATORS – WHAT DO YOU THINK OF THOSE TWO MEN?

INTERESTING. ESPECIALLY THE FAT ONE.

LET'S TRY IN HERE... IT MAY BE COOLER.

CALDARIVM

THIS WAS A FUNNY IDEA OF YOURS, ASTERIX, BY TOUTATIS!

HE SAID 'BY TOUTATIS' ... THEY'RE GAULS...

WE MAY BE HARD-BOILED, BUT THIS IS OVERDOING IT!

YOU SEEM TO BE STRANGERS HERE. I'LL GUIDE YOU ROUND THE BATHS. I COME HERE REGULARLY FOR MY HEALTH, THOUGH IT IS A BIT OF A SWEAT...

YOU SHOULD GO TO THE FRIGIDARIUM AND DIVE INTO THE POOL OF ICY WATER.

ICY WATER? I'M ON MY WAY!

WATCH ME DIVE, ASTERIX! WATCH ME DIVE!

16

20

21

YES, I DID HEAR ABOUT THE BARD THAT THE PREFECT OF GAUL GAVE CAESAR AS A PRESENT...

IT SEEMS THAT THIS BARD IS TO BE THROWN TO THE LIONS AT THE NEXT GAMES IN THE CIRCUS MAXIMUS, IN A FEW DAYS' TIME...

!!

WE'LL RESCUE HIM!

YOU CAN'T. THE BARD'S BEEN SHUT UP IN A CELL IN THE CIRCUS... AND IT'S A MAXIMUM SECURITY CIRCUS!

BUT THERE'S WORSE TO COME. THAT'S WHY I WARNED YOU TO BE CAREFUL. YOU MUST BE INDOMITABLE GAULS LIKE THE BARD! YOU MUST FLEE FROM ROME!

CAIUS FATUOUS, WHO TRAINS THE GLADIATORS, IS LOOKING FOR MEN FOR THE GAMES... AND INDOMITABLE GAULS ARE IN GREAT DEMAND!

WE WILL RESCUE OUR BARD!

YOU ACT THE FINE LADY AND YOU CAN'T EVEN AFFORD A SLAVE TO DO THE HOUSEWORK!

SO I AM A FINE LADY! SO YOU KNOW WHAT THE FINE LADY HAS TO SAY TO YOU?

BY JUNO, IF YOU DON'T SHUT UP I'M CALLING THE WATCH!

THESE ROMANS ARE CRAZY!

THERE THEY ARE!

WE'RE BEING ATTACKED!

GOODY!

LOOK, ASTERIX! I'VE THOUGHT OF SOMETHING NEW! LOOK, I DON'T EVEN TOUCH THEM, I SHAKE THEM! IT LASTS LONGER THAT WAY!

ALL RIGHT, OBELIX. PUT HIM DOWN NOW!

WILL YOU BE QUIET OUT THERE IN THE ROAD! WE CAN'T HEAR OURSELVES SHOUT IN HERE!

19

THIS INN OPPOSITE THE CIRCUS WILL SUIT US NICELY. LET'S SEE IF THEY HAVE ANY ROOM.

RIGHT.

CIRCUS INN

I WONDER IF THEY'LL LET US IN AT THIS TIME OF NIGHT...

I'LL JUST KNOCK...

SOON AFTERWARDS...

THAT WILL BE 20 SESTERTII FOR THE NIGHT AND 40 SESTERSII FOR THE DOOR.

MEANWHILE, IN THE HOUSE OF CAIUS FATUOUS THE GLADIATOR TRAINER...

WELL, DID YOU GET THEM?

ER... NO, BOSS... THEY DIDN'T WANT TO COME.

I MUST HAVE THOSE TWO MEN! JUMP TO IT, EVERYONE!

AND NEXT MORNING...

SLEEP WELL, ASTERIX?

YES, THANK YOU, OBELIX. LET'S GO AND HAVE BREAKFAST NOW.

WE MUST TRY TO GET INTO CONVERSATION WITH ONE OF THE CIRCUS GUARDS AND FIND OUT EXACTLY WHERE CACOFONIX IS IMPRISONED!

WAITER! HAVE YOU BY ANY CHANCE GOT SOME PARSLEY?

PARSLEY? WHAT FOR?

FOR PUTTING IN MY EARS! I'VE GOT A PRISONER WHO KEEPS ON SINGING, SOMETHING HORRIBLE!

THAT'S CACOFONIX!

THE DESCRIPTION FITS, ANYWAY!

20

26

28

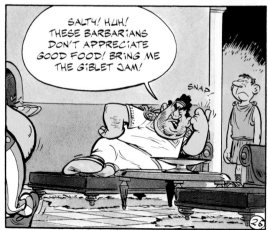

30

33

AND YOU GLADIATORS, GET BACK TO YOUR TRAINING. I HAVE TO GO AND SEE CAESAR...

I SAY, OBELIX, SUPPOSE WE TOOK A LITTLE STROLL ROUND TOWN TOO?

NOT A BAD IDEA!

HALT, GLADIATORS! YOU AREN'T ALLOWED OUT OF YOUR QUARTERS!

PUT THAT HELMET DOWN, OBELIX! YOU'LL HAVE TO GET OUT OF THAT SILLY HABIT!

WHAT FOR? IT DOESN'T HURT ANYONE!

THESE MODERN CITIES ARE ALL VERY WELL, BUT THEY'RE NOT WHAT I'D CALL FRIENDLY.

LET'S GO AND SEE WHAT'S HAPPENING OVER THERE WHERE ALL THOSE PEOPLE ARE READING THAT NOTICE.

MEANWHILE...

HERE'S THE PROGRAMME FOR THE GAMES, O CAESAR. I'VE HAD THESE TABLETS PUT UP ALL OVER ROME.

IF THE PEOPLE LIKE THE GAMES, I SHALL TREAT YOU GENEROUSLY. IF NOT, THE LIONS GET THE TREAT!

GRAND CIRCUS GAMES

IMPRESARIO, CAIUS FATUOUS

CHARIOT RACES

GAULISH BARD THROWN TO THE LIONS,

GLADIATORIAL CONTESTS WITH

ASTERIX & OBELIX

THE INDOMITABLE GAULS

(BOOKING OFFICE NOW OPEN)

NOT BAD... BUT YOU'D BETTER NOT LET THE GAULS ESCAPE. THEY'RE THE STAR ATTRACTION.

DON'T YOU WORRY, O CAESAR, THEY'RE SAFELY LOCKED AWAY!

AT LAST I'LL BE ABLE TO BUY THAT LITTLE FARM AT ALBUM IN THE PROVINCE OF STERNUM!

LOOK! IF IT ISN'T GOOD OLD FATUOUS!

?!

SO IT IS! THERE'S A BIT OF LUCK!

30

TIME PASSES BY, AND THE GLADIATORS ARE PUTTING ON WEIGHT...

MY FIRST IS A HUNDRED, MY SECOND IS A SIGN OF THE ZODIAC, MY THIRD IS A HIBERNIAN, MY FOURTH IS THE EGYPTIAN GOD OF THE SUN AND JULIUS CAESAR LOVES MY WHOLE! WHO AM I?

WHILE CAIUS FATUOUS IS LOSING IT...

THERE THEY GO AGAIN! PLAYING IDIOTIC GAMES INSTEAD OF TRAINING! A FINE CIRCUS THIS IS GOING TO BE!

IT'S C, LEO, PAT, RA... CLEOPATRA!

THAT WAS A DIFFICULT ONE, THAT WAS!

THE GAMES ARE FIXED FOR TOMORROW. THIS WILL BE YOUR LAST NIGHT IN THE CIRCUS, YOU USELESS LOT!

WE DON'T REALLY WANT TO FIGHT ANY MORE, ASTERIX.

DON'T WORRY! I PROMISE YOU WON'T HAVE TO RISK YOUR LIVES IN THE ARENA!

AND A VERY RELAXED GROUP OF GLADIATORS ARRIVES AT THE CIRCUS...

STOP PUSHING, WILL YOU!

HA, HA! HO, HO!

PORPUS IS A BEAST! PASS IT ON!

WHAT'S THE MATTER WITH THEM?

NO IDEA. LOCK THEM UP DOWN BELOW!

PORTER, WE WANT TO SEE OUR FRIEND CACOFONIX THE BARD.

I'M NOT A PORTER AND YOU CAN'T!

VERY WELL THEN, WE SHALL TEAR OUT THESE BARS ONE BY ONE UNTIL YOU CO-OPERATE!

GO AHEAD AND TRY!

PLINNNK!

PLONNNK!

PLUNNNK!

STOP! LEAVE THE FIXTURES ALONE!

AH, ABOUT TIME TOO! WHAT SERVICE!

32

37

A HUGE CROWD IS FORMING OUTSIDE THE CIRCUS...

WASH YOUR TOGAS IN SUPER PERSIC! SUPER PERSIC WASHES EVEN PURPLER!

SCORE CARD! SCORE CARD!

CUSHIONS! CUSHIONS!

CHIPOLATAE! CANES CALIDI! CHIPOLATAE!

AND INSIDE THE IMPOSING ARENA THE TRUMPETS ANNOUNCE THE ARRIVAL OF CAESAR IN THE IMPERIAL BOX...

TANTAN TARA!!!!

PANEM ET CIRCENSES

LONG LIVE CAESAR!

CAESAR FOR EVER!

EVERYONE APPLAUDS THE DICTATOR...

CLAP! CLAP! CLAP! CLAP! CLAP! CLAP! CLAP! CLAP!

ET TU BRUTE!*

CLAP! CLAP! CLAP!

CLAP! CLAP! CLAP! CLAP!

* YOU TOO, BRUTUS!

THAT BRUTUS... I CAN SEE I'M GOING TO HAVE TROUBLE WITH HIM.*

CLAP! CLAP! CLAP! CLAP! CLAP! CLAP! CLAP! CLAP!

* AN EXAMINATION OF ACT III, SCENE 1 OF JULIUS CAESAR BY WILLIAM SHAKESPEARE WILL INDICATE THE PROPHETIC NATURE OF THIS REMARK.

THIS WILL BE A GREAT SHOW, O CAESAR!

I HOPE SO, CAIUS FATUOUS. IF NOT, YOU'LL BE IN ON THE ACT.

LET THE GAMES BEGIN!

GULP!—

34

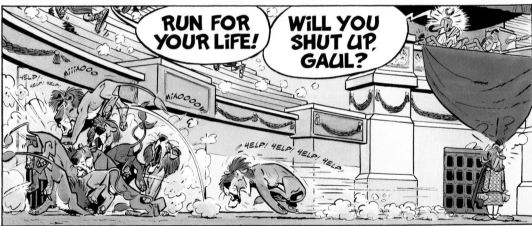

44

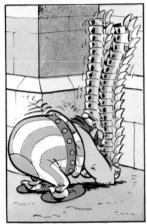

45

46

AND AFTER A FEW HOURS' WALK...

O EKONOMIKRISIS, PHOENICIAN MERCHANT, WILL YOU KEEP YOUR PROMISE AND TAKE US BACK TO GAUL?

MY OLD FRIENDS THE GAULS!!!

COME ABOARD, FRIENDS! BUSINESS WAS GOOD. I HAVE SOLD EVERYTHING, AND NOW I HAVE TO STOCK UP AGAIN!

WHO'S THIS?

A LITTLE SURPRISE FOR YOUR ROWING PARTNERS!

DO I ... DO I HAVE TO ROW ALL BY MYSELF? ALL THE WAY BACK TO GAUL?

THIS WILL TEACH YOU TO DO A DIRTY JOB AND LIVE OFF OTHER PEOPLE'S MUSCLE!

WHY DON'T I SING A LITTLE SOMETHING TO LIVEN HIM UP?

NOOOO!

HE'S GREAT!

WHAT AN OARSMAN!

HEAR, HEAR!

SPLAT! SPLAT! SPLAT! SPLAT! SPLAT! SPLAT!

I FEEL WE MIGHT MAKE THIS ROMAN A PARTNER!

AN EXCELLENT NOTION, MR. CHAIRMAN!

BAH!

THE VOYAGE IS UNEVENTFUL, EXCEPT FOR A SKIRMISH WITH THE PIRATES...

CHEER UP, CAP'N! WE'RE ALL IN THE SAME BOAT!

43

47

THE END